ALFIE

Alfie and the Big Boys

For all children who will soon be starting school

Other titles in the Alfie series:

Alfie Gets in First
Alfie's Feet
Alfie Gives a Hand
An Evening at Alfie's
Alfie and the Birthday Surprise
Alfie Wins a Prize
Alfie Weather
Alfie's World
Annie Rose is my Little Sister
Rhymes for Annie Rose
The Big Alfie and Annie Rose Storybook
The Big Alfie Out of Doors Storybook

ALFIE AND THE BIG BOYS
A RED FOX BOOK 978 1 849 41070 0

First published in Great Britain by The Bodley Head, an imprint of Random House Children's Books
A Random House Group Company

The Bodley Head edition published 2007
Red Fox edition published 2009
This edition published 2010 for Index Books Ltd

Copyright © Shirley Hughes, 2007

Red Fox Books are published by Random House Children's Books, 61–63 Uxbridge Road, London W5 5SA

www.kidsatrandomhouse.co.uk
www.rbooks.co.uk

Addresses for companies within The Random House Group Limited can be found at: www.randomhouse.co.uk/offices.htm

THE RANDOM HOUSE GROUP Limited Reg. No. 954009

A CIP catalogue record for this book is available from the British Library.

Printed in China

ALFIE

Alfie and the Big Boys

Shirley Hughes

Red Fox

In the mornings Alfie went to Nursery School. His friends Bernard, Min, Sara and Sam and the others went there too.

There were some
interesting things
to do at Nursery
School.

Alfie drew pictures and
learned how to write his
name at the top.

He did counting
and played
in the shop.

He sat on the floor with all the other children and listened to stories.

They sang songs together.

And sometimes they made
masks or paper crowns
to take home.

Alfie's Nursery School was right next door to the Big School, where Alfie and the others would go when they were older.

From their play area they could see the big children when they came out to play. Alfie and Bernard knew the names of some of the boys at Big School. There was Kevin Turley and Mohammed Rehan, Todd Rawlings and the Santos twins – who lived in Alfie's street. There was also a big boy with red hair whose name was Ian Barger.

Bernard liked Ian a lot, and laughed and laughed at the funny things he did. But Ian never took any notice of the little kids.

All the boys in Year One wanted to be in Ian's gang. Mostly they played football. Sometimes they pulled their sweaters over their heads and tore through the playground, hanging onto each other and pretending to be a fierce dragon.

They kept falling over on purpose and sometimes pulled other people over with them. Ian was always the one in front.

Bernard and Alfie both wished they could join in and be part of the fierce dragon too.

Alfie went to Nursery School on Monday, Tuesday, Wednesday, Thursday and Friday mornings. On Saturday and Sunday there was no school. Annie Rose was very pleased when Saturday morning came and Alfie could stay at home and play with her.

One fine Saturday morning Mum said she was going to take Alfie and Annie Rose with her to a pot plant sale. It was at a big house, not too far away. Alfie and Annie Rose had just started a good game and they didn't think pot plants sounded very interesting. But Dad was too busy to look after them that morning, so off they went.

The house where the pot plant sale was had a beautiful garden with shady paths and big trees and lots of flowers.

But Alfie and Annie Rose soon got bored with watching Mum choose pot plants.

Luckily, there was a grassy place at the end of the garden, where helpers were looking after some children who were playing on swings and a climbing frame and a slide. Mum asked Alfie if he would like to stay there for a little while and he said yes.

So Mum went off with Annie Rose, saying that they would be back very soon.

Alfie had not been there very long when a great commotion broke out. Somebody was screaming and yelling and making a terrible fuss.

All the helpers were crowded around.

Right in the middle of them was a boy with a runny nose and
tears pouring down his cheeks, yelling at the top of his voice.
"I want my mummy! I want my mummy!" he shouted.

The kind helpers were trying to comfort him but he just went on yelling, "I want my MUMMY!"

"Don't worry, we'll soon find her for you," said one.

"Tell us your name, dear, will you?" said another.

But the boy would not tell them his name. He was far too busy yelling and sobbing.

"Doesn't anyone know his name?" cried one helper.

Only one person knew who that boy was. And that person was Alfie.

"I know who he is," he told everybody. "His name is Ian Barger and he goes to Parkside School."

As soon as Ian caught sight of Alfie, he grabbed him and held onto him very tightly. Then, slowly, he stopped crying and began sniffing and hiccupping instead.

Just at that moment, who should come hurrying up, red in the face, but Ian's mum.

"Oh dear, oh dear, what a fuss!" she said. "I told you I would be just over there buying a pot of geraniums!" Then she gave Ian a big hug and wiped his nose. "Poor little Ian!" she said. "Did you think you had lost me when I was right over there all the time?" Ian nodded his head. He was still hiccupping and holding tightly onto Alfie's hand.

"Well, I see you had a kind friend to look after you so you needn't have been frightened, need you, sweetheart?" said Ian's mum. And she beamed at Alfie.

Then she thanked the helpers and thanked Alfie specially for taking care of Ian. "How lucky you were here!" she told him.

Afterwards, she and Alfie's mum
had a chat. When it was time to
go, she bought all three
children ice creams. Ian was
now holding onto her hand
very firmly indeed.

At school next Monday morning Ian came swaggering out to play with the other boys, as usual. And, as usual, he took no notice of Alfie and Bernard. But when the ball bounced over into their bit of the playground and Alfie threw it back, he said, "Thanks, mate!"

Alfie's mum became friendly with Ian's mum while they waited together outside the school gates. One day Mum invited her to bring Ian for tea after school. Bernard was invited too.

"Better lock up all the breakables!" said Dad when he heard that Bernard *and* Ian were coming to tea.

But, as it turned out, Ian
did not break anything at all.
He spent most of his time
playing with Annie Rose.
He helped her to line up
her dolls and cuddly toys
into a football team and she
told him all their names.
Then they made a house
for them out of cushions.

Bernard and Alfie thought
that was a very babyish game.

But after tea they all went outside and had a great game together being big, tough boys!